USBORNE HOTSHOTS

AMAZING FACTS

USBORNE HOTSHOTS

AMAZING FACTS

Edited by Alastair Smith
Designed by Nigel Reece

Illustrated by Ian Jackson,
Chris Shields and Guy Smith

Series editor: Judy Tatchell
Series designer: Ruth Russell

Additional illustrations by Gary Bines,
David Wright, Kuo Kang Chen, Peter Dennis,
Tony Gibson, John Lawrence, Allan Robinson,
John Shackell and Peter Wingham

CONTENTS

4 Galactic fact file

6 Our fantastic planet

8 Plant power

10 Amazing animals

12 Animal surprises

14 Feathered facts

16 Facts from the deep

18 Fishy facts

20 Nation information

22 Just look at you!

24 Brilliant body facts

26 Can you believe it?

28 Fantastic feats

30 The amazing quiz

32 Quiz answers

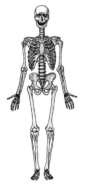

Galactic fact file

Sun

Venus

Earth

Mars

Mercury

Jupiter

Saturn

Uranus

Neptune

In our Solar System there are nine planets revolving around one star, the Sun.

Pluto

The Sun

The Sun is about a thousand times bigger than Jupiter (the biggest planet in our Solar System) and a million times bigger than the Earth.

By Jupiter!

Jupiter is over a thousand times bigger than the Earth. It is bigger than all the other eight planets of the Solar System put together.

Longest journey

It takes Pluto, the most distant planet in the Solar System, 248 years to go once around the Sun.

Living planet

As far as we know, Earth is the only planet where things can live. If it was any closer to or farther from the Sun, it would be too hot or cold for living things.

How far?

The Sun is 150 million km (93 million miles) from the Earth. If you could drive there, at 90kmph (55mph) it would take you 193 years to get there.

Pipsqueak planet

Pluto is the smallest and lightest planet in the Solar System. It is even smaller than our Moon. It can only be seen from Earth with the help of a telescope.

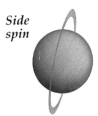

Uranus spins on its side, rolling like a giant wheel. Some scientists think that a huge comet hit it, tipping it sideways.

Saturn's rings appear to be solid, but in fact they are made of millions of ice particles, specks of dust and pieces of rock. Winds of 1,770kmph (1,100mph), ten times stronger than the worst hurricane on Earth, whistle around Saturn's equator.

Hot Mercury

Mountains and canyons

The planet Mercury is closest to the Sun. It has temperatures of up to 350°C (660°F). This is seven times hotter than any recorded temperature on the Earth.

One of the highest mountains in the Solar System is called Maxwell Montes, on planet Venus. It is over 2,000m (6,560ft) higher than the Earth's highest mountain, Mount Everest – which is 8,848m (29,028ft) high.

The biggest canyon in the entire Solar System is on Mars. It is 13 times longer than the longest canyon on Earth, the Grand Canyon in the USA.

The Milky Way

Our Solar System forms part of a galaxy, called the Milky Way. The Sun is just one of about 100,000 million stars in the Milky Way. There are millions of galaxies in space.

The Milky Way

Our fantastic planet

Temperatures

The coldest place is in Antarctica, with an average temperature of -56°C (-72°F). The hottest place is in Ethiopia, Africa, with an average temperature of 34°C (94°F).

Biggest desert

The biggest desert is the Sahara, in northern and central Africa. It is nearly as big as the USA.

Driest place

The Atacama desert in Chile is the driest desert on Earth. Parts of the desert had no rain for 400 years, from 1570-1971. In other parts rain has never been recorded.

Largest dunes

The world's largest sand dunes are in the Sahara desert. Some are up to 430m (1,420ft) high.

Iciest place

The continent of Antarctica is completely covered by a sheet of ice that is 1½ times bigger than the USA. About nine-tenths of all the world's ice is found there.

Longest river

The longest river in the world is the Nile, in Africa. It is about 6,600km (4,100 miles) long.

Covered in ice

Glaciers, huge masses of ice and snow, cover about one-tenth of the Earth's land surface, an area the size of South America. If all the glaciers were put together they would contain enough ice to cover the Earth with a layer 30m (98ft) thick.

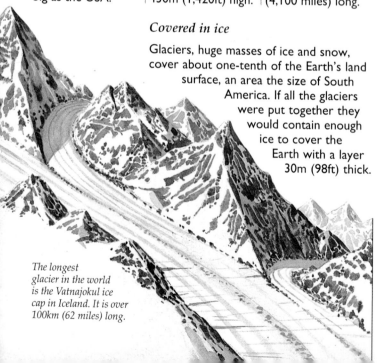

The longest glacier in the world is the Vatnajokul ice cap in Iceland. It is over 100km (62 miles) long.

If the ice melted

If all the ice on Earth melted it would raise the sea level by about 60m (200ft). Many coastal cities would be completely flooded, including New York City in the USA, and Sydney in Australia.

Mega lake

One-fifth of all the fresh water on Earth is held in just one lake, Lake Baikal in Russia.

Highest cliffs

The highest sea cliffs in the world are on the north coast of the island of Hawaii. They are a towering 1,005m (3,300ft) high – which is about the same height as a 275-floor tower block.

Disaster zone

China has the worst record for deaths from earthquakes. In 1556, an earthquake killed 830,000 people.

Highest peaks

There are 109 mountains that are over 7,320m (24,000ft) high. Of these, 96 are in the Himalayas in Asia. The highest mountain on Earth is Mount Everest. It reaches a height of 8,848m (29,028ft).

Water in the air

If all the water in the atmosphere fell as rain at once it could cover the Earth with 2.5cm (1in) of water.

Lively volcanoes

On average, between 20 and 30 volcanoes erupt every year. A few volcanoes, such as the volcanic island of Stromboli in Italy, erupt almost all of the time.

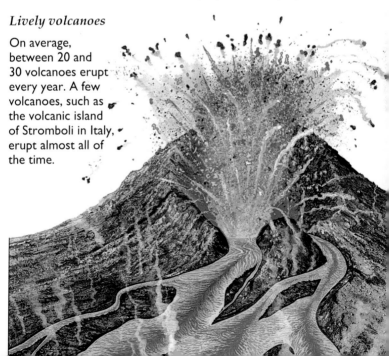

Plant power

Skyscraper cactus

A giant saguaro cactus can grow up to 15m (50ft) tall and live for over 200 years. A fully grown plant can weigh almost as much as two elephants.

Giant trees

The Earth's largest trees, giant sequoias, grow in forests in North America. Some have arches cut in their trunks that are big enough to drive a car through.

Ancient tree

The oldest living tree in the world is in California, USA. It is over 4,700 years old.

Float on

Coconuts that fall in the sea have floated for up to 2,000km (1,250 miles) before growing into new trees when they reach dry land.

Explosive fruit

When the fruits of the squirting cucumber plant are ripe, they burst open, shooting their seeds up to 8m (26ft) away from the plant. The seeds travel as fast as 100kmph (60mph).

Light giving

At night, parts of the Indian Ocean sparkle with light. The light is made by dinoflagellates – tiny sea plants. Millions of them together can give off enough light to read a book by.

Grass growing

There are about 10,000 different kinds of grass on the Earth.

Rice again

Rice is a type of grass. It is the only grass which can grow in water, and is the main food of more than half the world's population.

Big and smelly

The largest flower in the world grows on the rafflesia plant. It is the only part of the plant that appears above the ground. The flower smells of rotting meat.

Puffball bonanza

An average-sized giant puffball is 30cm (12in) across and can produce seven million million spores. In the right conditions, each spore could grow into a mature puffball.

Slow flower

The rare Bolivian *Puya raimondii* plant flowers only once in its 150 year life.

Firework moss

The spore cases of the stag's horn clubmoss produce a bright yellow powder, which was used at one time to make fireworks.

Meat eater

The sundew plant eats meat. It has sticky tentacles covering its leaves, which trap insects that land on the leaves. As the insects struggle to escape, the tentacles curl over and glue them firmly to the leaf so the plant can start digesting its meal.

Smallest plants

Diatoms are the smallest of all plants on the Earth. They are so miniscule that about 2,500 of them would be able to fit along the line that is printed below this paragraph.

Tasty orchid

The taste in some kinds of vanilla ice cream comes from a type of orchid.

Largest forests

The largest area of forest in the world is in Siberia, in northern Russia. A quarter of all the Earth's forests are there.

Amazing animals

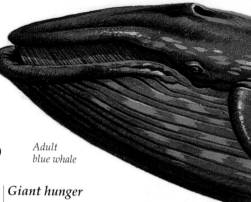

Largest animal

The largest animal on Earth is the blue whale. Adults can reach 34m (110ft) in length and weigh 190 tonnes (187 tons).

Adult blue whale

Loudest animal

The blue whale is the loudest of all animals. The noises it makes can be heard 850km (530 miles) away.

Giant hunger

In spring and summer a blue whale eats up to 4,000kg (nearly four tons) of food in a day. That is twice as much as a well fed person eats in a whole year. Its food consists entirely of tiny shrimp-like animals called krill.

Kissy-kissy

When two prairie dogs meet at the entrance to a nest they give each other a sort of kiss to find out if they recognize each other.

Sure-footed

Rocky mountain goats have hollows in their hooves which stick to rocks like suction pads. They can climb near-vertical slopes easily.

Rousing chorus

To warn off enemies, howler monkeys get together and howl so loud that the din can be heard about 8km (5 miles) away.

Smelly skunk

The terrible smell a skunk makes when it is threatened comes from a gland under its tail. The vile stink can waft for up to 0.5km (0.3 mile).

Busy beaver

Using its bare teeth, a beaver can fell a tree 50cm (20in) thick in just 15 minutes. Beavers use felled trees to build places to live.

Getting clean

Some types of giant tortoises allow finches to clean them. They stretch their necks and legs so the birds can take insects from under their shells.

Compare the sizes

The biggest land animal of all is the African elephant. An adult male can reach around 4m (13ft) in height. The picture above shows the African elephant's size in proportion to a blue whale.

Vampires!

Vampire bats suck blood from other animals, but they don't need much. Even the biggest ones only need a tablespoonful a day.

Dirty sloth

Sloths are so dirty that green algae grow on their coats. Moths lay eggs on the algae. When the caterpillars hatch they eat the algae.

Big little eater

Etruscan shrews eat three times their own weight per day. A man would have to eat a sheep, 50 hens, 60 loaves and 150 apples to match this.

Big eyes

Eastern tarsiers have huge eyes. If your eyes were as big compared with your head, they would be the size of grapefruits.

Clever monkey

To cope with the cold in the northern Japanese mountains where they live, macaque monkeys bathe in hot pools of volcanic spring water.

Interesting tail

Spider monkeys have such strong tails that they can use them to support their whole body weight. More often, though, they use their tails like an extra arm.

11

Animal surprises

Flying mammals

The only mammals that can fly are bats. The biggest bat is the flying fox, with a wing span of around 183cm (6ft).

Small fact

The smallest breed of horse is the falabella. Adults grow to less than 30cm (12in) in height.

Big teeth

Elephants keep growing teeth until they are about 45 years old. Their final teeth each weigh about 4kg (9lb) – about the same weight as a new-born human.

Giant panda facts

Most giant pandas live in the mountains of China. They eat bamboo. The word *panda* comes from the Nepalese language and means "bamboo eater".

Fastest

Cheetahs are the fastest of all land mammals. They have a top speed of approximately 115kmph (75mph).

Little monkey

Adult pygmy marmoset monkeys are 14cm (6in) tall – less than the height of this book.

Giant eater

The South American giant anteater has a 60cm (24in) long tongue, which it uses to catch its main food – ants. Anteaters can eat well over 30,000 ants in a single day.

Big nose

The nose of the proboscis monkey keeps growing all its life. An old male's nose can be 18cm (7in) long. *Proboscis* means "nose" in Greek.

Smallest dog

The smallest ever dog was a Yorkshire terrier. It was 6.3cm (2.5in) tall and weighed about as much as a hamster.

Mini mammal

The smallest land mammals, Savi's pygmy shrews, weigh about as much as table-tennis balls.

Ancient ape

The oldest ape ever known was a male orangutan called Guas. He died in 1977 at the grand old age of 57. Guas the ape lived at the Philadelphia Zoo in Pennsylvania, USA.

Slow coach

The sloth is the slowest land mammal, with a top speed of 2kmph (1.3 mph). Normally it would take a sloth 22 minutes to travel 100m (110yd).

High table

A giraffe's tongue is about 45cm (18in) long (about as long as an adult human's thigh). The tongue is also very strong. A giraffe will wrap it around thick tree branches, and then yank the branches down to mouth level so that it can eat the tasty leaves.

Tallest

Giraffes are the tallest mammals on Earth. An adult male Masai giraffe can grow to over 5m (17ft) tall. The tallest ever giraffe on record measured a lofty 5.87m (19.25ft). This is taller than the combined heights of three men.

Giant rodent

Capybaras are the world's largest rodents (rat-like animals). They are about the size of sheep. Capybaras live in river banks in Central and South America.

Most poisonous

The marine cobra's venom is the most poisonous in the world. It is about 100 times more potent than any other snake's. Marine cobras live in the seas around north Australia.

The high life

Yaks live higher up from sea level than any other mammal. Yaks have been spotted at an altitude of 6,100m (20,000ft) in the Himalayas.

Water babies

Hippopotamuses are born underwater. A baby hippopotamus knows how to swim as soon as it is born. *Hippopotamus* is a Greek word meaning "river horse".

Feathered facts

Removable beak

Puffins are the only birds whose beaks change depending on the time of year. During the mating season they grow eye-catching beaks so that they can attract a mate. Later in the year the outer layer is shed, leaving them with smaller, duller beaks.

Puffin during the mating season

Millions of birds

There are around 100,000 million birds in the world. Of these, about 3,000 million are domestic chickens.

Smelly sea bird

Fulmars defend their nests from attackers by spitting a foul-smelling oil from their stomachs at intruders.

Too fat to fly

Baby gannets eat so much fish that they become massively fat. When they leave the nest they starve until they are light enough to fly.

Phoenix fowl

The phoenix fowl's tail feathers are fantastically long. The longest ones ever recorded were about the same length as a bus.

Breakout

Most baby birds take 30 minutes to an hour to hatch out, but albatross chicks need up to six days to get out of their tough shells.

Giant babies

Some birds are at their heaviest when they are very young. A young wandering albatross can weigh up to 16kg (35lb). Its weight has dropped to about 11kg (24lb) by the time it has learned to fly properly.

Biggest wings

The wandering albatross has the greatest wingspan – up to 3.7m (12ft) from wingtip to wingtip. The combined length of two average-sized people would be less than this.

Marathon flyer

The arctic tern travels farther than any other bird. Twice a year it flies from one polar region to the other. The combined distance of these journeys is around 40,000km (25,000 miles).

Dangerous life

Most birds are at constant risk. About three-quarters of all wild birds die before they reach six months old. Other animals and human hunters present two of the biggest threats.

Smallest bird

The smallest bird in the world is the bee hummingbird. It is around 3cm (1.25in) long. It weighs less than some insects.

Largest nest

The largest nest on record was built by bald eagles in Florida, USA. It was 2.9m (9.5ft) wide and 6m (20ft) deep. It weighed over 2,000kg (4,400lb), which is about as much as two jeeps.

Egg record

An American redhead duck's nest was found with 87 eggs inside. Lots of ducks had used the same nest.

Flamingo pink

In the wild, a flamingo eats lots of shrimps, which make its feathers pink. If it doesn't eat this food its feathers go dull. In captivity flamingos are often fed carrot juice to keep their feathers bright.

The oldest bird

The oldest known bird was a great sulphur-crested cockatoo who lived to the age of about 82. He died in 1982.

Almighty ostrich

The African ostrich is the largest bird. Males can be 2.7m (9ft) tall and weigh up to 156kg (345lb), about twice as much as a man.

Largest egg

Ostriches lay the largest eggs of any bird. Their eggs measure about 15-20cm (6-8in) long and weigh around 1.7kg (3.7lb). The shell is strong enough to support the weight of a very large man, about 127kg (280lb).

Ostriches can be trained to herd sheep and to scare other birds away from crops.

Facts from the deep

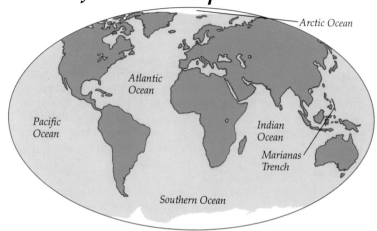

Arctic Ocean

Atlantic Ocean

Pacific Ocean

Indian Ocean

Marianas Trench

Southern Ocean

Watery Earth

Over two-thirds of the Earth is covered by sea water. This lies in the Pacific, Atlantic, Indian, Arctic and Southern Oceans. Oceans contain 97% of all the Earth's water. The rest is in ice, rivers and lakes.

Black smokers

In parts of the Pacific Ocean, mineral-rich hot water seeps up through cracks in the ocean floor. The minerals form "chimney stacks" as tall as houses around the cracks.

Giant ocean

The Pacific Ocean is the biggest ocean of all. It covers almost one-third of the Earth's surface, and almost half of all the seas. At its widest point, it stretches nearly halfway around the world.

Gold mine

There is a huge amount of gold in the seas around the world. If all of it could be brought ashore, there would be enough for each person on Earth to have a piece that weighed 1kg (2.2lb).

Still growing

The Atlantic, the second largest of all the oceans, is still growing. Each year, it grows about 4cm (1.5in) wider, gradually pushing the continents of Europe and North America farther and farther apart.

Sea level

The sea level does not always stay the same. 18,000 years ago, during the last Ice Age, the sea level was around 120m (400ft) lower than now. It was possible to walk between England and France.

Deep sea carpet

Most of the deep ocean floor is caked in ooze up to 10km (6 miles) thick, made of dead plants and animals, and mud.

Tsunami terrors

Undersea volcanoes and earthquakes can trigger tsunamis, giant waves which rear up to 30m (100ft), swamping whole islands.

Monster iceberg

The biggest iceberg ever seen covered an area larger than the European country of Belgium. It was seen in 1956.

Sea salt

If all the salt in the sea was removed and spread over the Earth's land surface, it would make up a layer of salt around 150m (500ft) thick.

Going down

The deepest part of all the oceans is the Marianas Trench in the Pacific Ocean. It is 11,034m (36,200ft) deep.

How much salt?

The amount of salt in sea water varies. The Red Sea (between east Africa and Saudi Arabia) has six times as much salt as the Baltic Sea in Europe.

Coral reefs

Corals grow in warm, tropical waters. Coral reefs are the skeletons of billions of tiny corals. More sea creatures live around coral reefs than in any other part of the ocean.

There are thousands of different species of corals that form different shapes, such as fine sea fans, "brain" shapes and massive boulders.

Sea fan

Emperor angel fish live and eat around coral reefs.

Clown fish hide in coral reefs.

Fishy facts

Deep-sea anglerfish

Sea monster

The deep-sea anglerfish has a light-emitting stalk that grows just above its mouth. In the dark depths of the sea the light attracts prey within range of its huge, fang-filled mouth.

Escape

A captured starfish can escape from its attacker by leaving some of its arms behind. All starfish can grow new arms. A re-grown starfish can end up with as many as nine arms instead of the usual five.

Pistol packer

The pistol shrimp makes good use of its large right claw. It snaps the claw to make a sound like a pistol shot. The sound sends shock waves that stun small fish nearby. Then it moves in to eat the stunned fish.

Danger, cucumber!

If a sea cucumber is threatened by a hungry fish, it shoots out streams of sticky threads. The threads entangle the fish like a gooey lasso and give the sea cucumber time to make a quick getaway.

Helpful fish

Cleaner fish clean pests and dead skin off the bodies of larger fish. They work inside the gills and mouths as well as over the bodies of their patients.

Fish out of water

The four-winged flying fish has been seen flying out of water for about 90 seconds, soaring to heights of 11m (36ft), almost twice as high as a giraffe.

Blow out

When the porcupine fish is surprised by an attacker, it gulps in water and blows up to soccer-ball size. This causes sharp spines all over its body to stick out.

Shark facts

Whale sharks are the world's largest fish. They can grow to over 18m (60ft) long and weigh six times more than the biggest land animals, African elephants.

Hitching a ride

Remoras hitch rides from other fish by sticking to them using a sucker on top of their heads. When the host finds food, the remora eats up the scraps.

Garden of eels

Garden eels live, tail down, in holes in the sand on the sea bed. They poke their bodies up out of the holes and wait to grab food as it drifts by into their reach.

Eyes surprise

One type of deep sea squid is born with both eyes the same size, but as it gets older its right eye grows up to four times bigger than its left eye. Nobody is certain why this happens to the squid.

Biggest crab

The biggest type of crab in the world is the Japanese spider crab. The most monstrously massive one ever found measured 3.7m (just over 12ft) across its front claws. A hippo would be able to fit between them.

Sinister stones

Stonefish have double protection from enemies. They are well-camouflaged, looking like weed-covered rocks. They also have 13 sharp spines on their backs, to inject deadly poison into things that press on them.

Fast fish

The fastest fish, the sailfish, can speed along at 109kmph (68mph) – faster than a cheetah, the fastest land animal. At high speed, its sail-like back fin slots into a groove on its back, making it superbly streamlined.

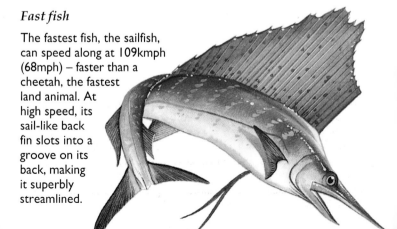

Nation information

Massive coast

Canada's coast is 250,000km (155,000 miles) long. If it was straightened out it would stretch around the world more than six times.

Greenland

Greenland is the world's biggest island, but its population is smaller than a small town's.

Smallest country

The world's smallest country is called Vatican City. It has a population of just 1,000 people.

GREENLAND

CANADA

USA

MEXICO

VATICAN CITY is in Rome, Italy

The continent of AFRICA

THE GAMBIA

BRAZIL

Most roads

The USA has more roads than any other country. It has well over 6 million km (3¾ million miles) of roads.

Mega city

About one-fifth of all the 83 million people in Mexico live in the capital city, Mexico City. This has made it one of the biggest cities in the world, with a population of over 15 million people.

Brazil

There are 143 million people in Brazil. They all speak Portuguese. There are more Portuguese speakers in Brazil than in Portugal, where the language originated.

Africa

There are 49 countries in Africa. The biggest of these is Sudan. It is 220 times bigger than the smallest African country, the Gambia.

Largest country

The largest country in the world is the Russian Federation. It has a total area of about 17,000 million square km (6,600 million square miles).

Most people

The country with the most people is China. It has a population of over 1,000 million. That is about one-fifth of all the people in the whole world.

Fans of fish

Japanese people eat the most fish. On average, they each eat 30kg (65lb) of fish a year. The Japanese eat twice as much fish as the Norwegians, the second biggest fish eaters.

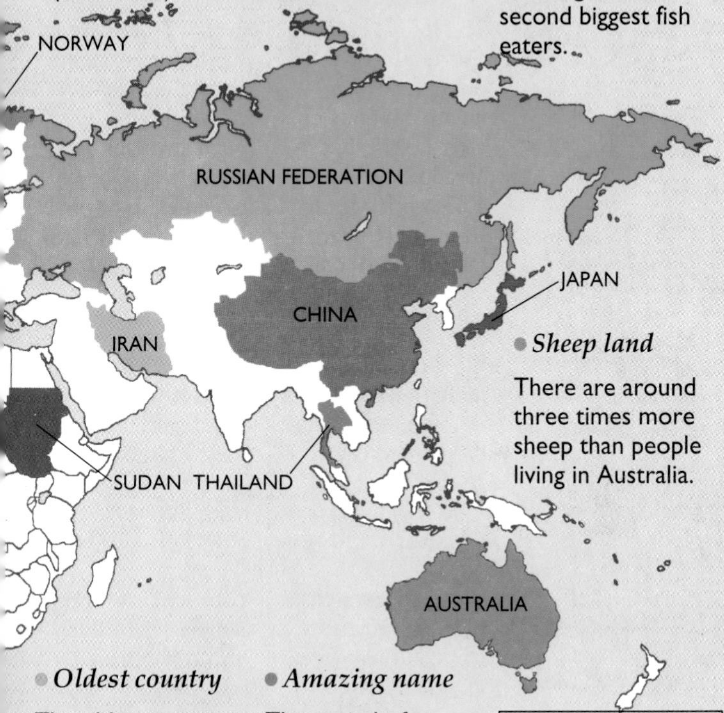

NORWAY

RUSSIAN FEDERATION

JAPAN

CHINA

IRAN

Sheep land

There are around three times more sheep than people living in Australia.

SUDAN THAILAND

AUSTRALIA

Oldest country

The oldest country in the world is Iran (or Persia as it used to be known). It has been an independent country for around 2,600 years, since the 6th century BC.

Amazing name

The capital of Thailand, Krung Thep (also known as Bangkok) has a full name that is 167 letters long. The English translation is shown here.

The City of Gods, the Great City, the Residence of the Emerald Buddha, the Impregnable City (of Ayutthaya) of God Indra, the grand capital of the world endowed with nine precious gems, the happy city, abounding in an enormous Royal Palace which resembles the heavenly abode where reigns the reincarnated god, a city given by Indra and built by Vishnukaru.

Just look at you!

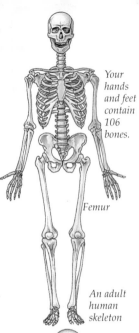

Your hands and feet contain 106 bones.

Femur

An adult human skeleton

Bone facts

At birth you have 300 bones. Some fuse together as you grow. Adults only have 206 bones.

The longest bone is the femur, or thigh bone. Its exact length depends on your height, but in an adult measuring 1.83m (6ft), it can be around 50cm (about 20in) long.

Your smallest bone is in your ear. It is called the stapes, or stirrup, and it is only 3mm (0.12in) long.

Bone is much lighter than concrete or steel but, weight for weight, it is much stronger. For example, a bone is five times stronger than a steel bar of the same weight.

Muscle facts

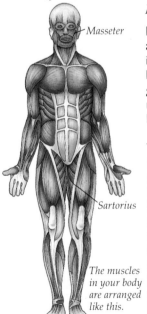

Masseter

Sartorius

The muscles in your body are arranged like this.

Most people have about 640 muscles in their bodies. The biggest are the gluteus maximus muscles in your buttocks and thighs.

The smallest muscle in your body is the stapedius, which is in your ear. It is less than 0.13cm (0.05in) long. The stapedius controls the movements of the smallest bone in your body, the stapes, or stirrup bone.

Your strongest muscles (called the masseters) enable you to bite with a force that is the same as the weight of 18 house bricks.

Your longest muscle is the sartorius. It runs down from your pelvis to your knee. It helps you to cross your legs. Its name comes from a Latin word *sartor*, which means "tailor". In the past, tailors often sat cross-legged to sew.

Heart beat

Your heart beats about 100,000 times a day. This means that if you live for 75 years, your heart will beat more than 2.5 billion times.

Breathing

In a normal breath, you take in about three cupfuls of air. In a day, an adult breathes enough air to fill up about a thousand party balloons.

Watery body

Up to two-thirds of your body weight is made up of water. This means that you contain enough water to fill about 1½ large buckets.

Feeling hungry?

In your lifetime, you will eat around 30,000kg (66,138lb) of food. That is equal to the weight of six elephants.

Blood red

Blood is red because it contains red blood cells. Red blood cells are so tiny that there are 25 million of them in every teaspoonful of blood.

How much?

Each day you pass enough urine to fill a large bottle. At this rate you can expect to expel enough urine to fill 500 bathtubs during your lifetime.

Shrinking

As adults grow older they shrink. By the time they are 75 they may be around 7cm (3in) shorter than they were at the age of 20.

Swallow this

Swallowed food travels through 3.5m (11.5ft) of pipes and tubes inside your body, a distance as long as a car.

Red blood cells, magnified many times

Buckets of blood

At rest your heart pumps about a third of a cup of blood with every beat. At that rate it would take about 3¾ minutes to fill a bucket with blood.

Hairy!

The longest hair ever recorded was grown by a monk in India. In 1949 his hair was measured at 8m (26ft) – over 13 times longer than your arm.

Choppers

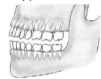

Most people grow two sets of teeth in their life. However, a few people grow a third or fourth set when they are old.

Brilliant body facts

Budding tasters

Your tongue is covered with tiny sensitive areas called taste buds. These detect four main tastes – sweet, sour, salty and bitter. You have over 10,000 taste buds but some die as you get older.

Different parts of your tongue pick up different tastes, as shown in the picture on the right.

Salty
Sweet
Sour
Bitter

Fingernails

Your fingernails grow by about 0.05cm (0.02in) per week – about 2m (6.5ft) in 75 years. A man in India grew one of his nails for nearly 40 years until it had reached over 1m (about 40in) in length.

Sneeze speed

Sneezing is something that you do automatically to clear slimy mucus or dust from your nose. You normally breathe air out at about 8kmph (5mph). In a sneeze, air travels at over 160kmph (100mph).

Sweat facts

Sweat is made by sweat glands in your skin. You have over 3 million sweat glands. Even on a cold day you lose a large cupful of sweat through your skin. On a hot day you lose enough to fill a large bottle.

Skin shade fact

Skin shade depends on how much of a brown-black pigment, called melanin, it has. Dark skin contains more than light skin. Melanin protects skin from sunburn.

Tiny mites

Some people have tiny, harmless, spider-like mites living in the hair follicles of their eyelashes. The mites are just 0.3mm (0.01in) long.

Temperature

Your normal body temperature is 37°C (98.6°F). You can die if it falls below 25°C (77°F). Some lucky people have survived with temperatures of 16°C (60.8°F).

Skin facts

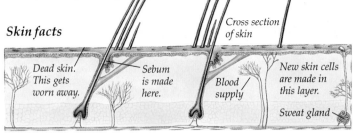

Cross section of skin

Dead skin. This gets worn away.

Sebum is made here.

Blood supply

New skin cells are made in this layer.

Sweat gland

Your thickest skin, on the soles of your feet, is about 6mm (0.25in) thick. Most of your skin is about 2mm (0.08in) thick.

Apart from on your fingers and toes, your skin makes itself waterproof by producing an oily film, called sebum.

You lose millions of skin cells and hundreds of hairs every day. In a year, you lose 2kg (4.5lb) of skin and hair.

Brain facts

Different parts of your brain control different things, as shown in the picture below. On average, the human brain weighs about 1.4kg (3lb). The heaviest one ever recorded weighed about 2kg (4.5lb).

Each half of your brain controls the opposite side of your body. In right-handed people, the left half of your brain controls writing and speech. In left-handed people the right half is in charge.

Your brain needs a constant supply of blood to give it enough oxygen and nutrients to keep it going properly. If too little blood reaches your brain, you feel faint. Your brain cells die after five minutes without oxygen.

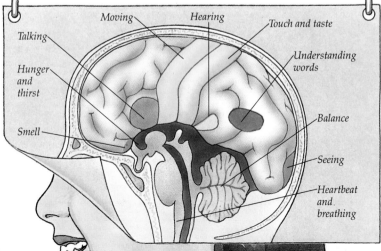

Moving

Hearing

Touch and taste

Talking

Understanding words

Hunger and thirst

Balance

Smell

Seeing

Heartbeat and breathing

Can you believe it?

Marble marvel

The Taj Mahal was built for the Indian emperor Shah Jahan as a tomb for his wife. It took 20 years to finish. On its completion the emperor had the architect's head cut off to stop him from designing a more beautiful building.

Happy birthday

The oldest person ever recorded is Jeanne Louise Calment. She was born in France on February 21 1875. When this book was written she was still alive – aged 121. When World War II began she was 69.

Healthy eater

The Ethiopian ruler, Emperor Manelik II, believed that eating pages from the Bible would cure him if he was ill. In 1913, to help him recover from illness, he ate a large section page by page. A few days later he died.

X-ray eyes?

In the 1930s, a man from New York City claimed he could see without using his eyes. To prove his point he rode blindfold on a bike through heavy traffic without crashing. Nobody knows how he did this.

Picture writing

The first people to write things down were the Sumerians, who lived in an area that is now Iraq. Their writing used pictures, not letters.

Tea guzzlers

British people drink more tea than any other nationality. They drink the equivalent of 1,355 cups per person every year.

A big load

The Great Pyramid in Egypt took 30 years to build and contains enough stone to build a wall 3m (10ft) high around France.

Beetle power

For its size, the rhinoceros beetle is extremely strong. It can carry 850 times its own weight on its back. To match this a human would have to carry eight African elephants.

Survivor

In 1972, Vesna Vulovic, an air stewardess from Yugoslavia, survived a fall of 10,000m (33,000ft) when the plane she was working in was blown up. Her fall was broken by landing in a pond.

Mighty builders

Termites are only the size of rice grains, but in groups they build massive nests. Using mud and saliva they build nests up to 6m (20ft) tall and 30m (100ft) wide.

Another survivor

In 1930, a German pilot bailed out of his glider and passed through a storm cloud as he fell. In the cloud he was coated with ice. The ice formed a giant hailstone around him, which broke his fall when he landed.

Giant snowman

In 1988 a group of people in Alaska, USA, spent two weeks building Super Frosty, the biggest snowman. It stood over 19m (62ft) high, even taller than a six-floor building.

Supermother

A Russian woman had a grand total of 69 children between the years 1725 and 1765. Her babies included 16 pairs of twins, seven sets of triplets and four sets of quadruplets (four babies born at the same birth).

Wonder wall

The biggest wall in the world is the Great Wall of China. It is about 3,460km (2,150 miles) long, with about 2,860km (1,780 miles) of branches. In total it is nearly as long as the Nile, the world's longest river.

Fantastic feats

It's a goal!

Usually, there are two or three goals in a first-class soccer match. However, in a match in Scotland in 1885, Arbroath beat Bon Accord by 36-0.

Super climber

In 1986, Italian Reinhold Messner became the first person to climb all of the world's 14 mountains over 8,000m (26,250ft).

Super athlete

In 1935, US athlete Jesse Owens set six world records in 45 minutes. This is a record in itself.

Solo sailor

The first person to sail solo around the world was Joshua Slocum, between 1895 and 1898. The daring sailor took quite a risk – he could not swim.

High divers

Professional high divers in Acapulco, Mexico, dive head first from a height of 27m (88ft) into the sea at a point where it is only 3.5m (12ft) deep.

Locked up

In 1835 an Indian fakir (Hindu holy man) was locked into a chest and buried underground. 40 days later the fakir emerged alive.

Champions

Brazil has won the most World Cup soccer victories – four, in 1958, 1962, 1970 and 1994.

The golden set

In tennis, a golden set is won when a player wins without conceding a point. Only Bill Scanlon has done this during a professional match, in 1983.

Over a barrel

In 1901, Anna Edson Taylor became the first person to ride over Niagara Falls in a barrel. She was badly shaken by her 54m (160ft) drop, but she survived.

Most on a bike

In 1987, 46 people managed to get on one motorbike. The riders managed to stay on the bike for a distance of 1.6km (1 mile).

Shortest fight

In 1946 boxer Ralph Walton was knocked out after just 10½ seconds of his fight against Al Couture.

Tightrope walker

Venezuela

South America

In 1988 Frenchman Michel Menin made the highest tightrope walk. He crossed Angel Falls, Venezuela, 1,008m (3,304ft) above the ground.

First cycle race

The first cycle race was held in Paris on May 31, 1868. It was won by an Englishman, James Moore. He rode an early type of bicycle called a velocipede, like the one shown here.

Most famous race

The *Tour de France* is held every year. Cyclists from all over the world race for about 3,000km (2,000 miles) around France. More than 10 million people line the route to watch the race, the biggest audience for any sporting event.

Most bikes

China is thought to have an estimated 20 million cyclists — more than any other country.

The Olympic Games

The first Olympics were held in Greece in 776BC. They were stopped in AD393 on the orders of a Roman Emperor and were not restarted until 1896, when they took place in Athens.

The most individual gold medals won at an Olympic Games is seven, won by Mark Spitz (USA) in 1972.

The Olympic Games are held every four years. Only a few countries have been represented at every single Games since 1896. They are Australia, Greece, France, Great Britain and Switzerland.

The amazing quiz

You can use this quiz to test your knowledge of the amazing information that is in this book. Score one point for each correct answer. The answers are on page 32.

1. Which country has more Portuguese speakers, Portugal or Brazil?

2. The word *hippopotamus* means: a) "massive mouth"; b) "river horse"; c) "water baby".

3. The smallest bone and the smallest muscle are in the same part of your body. Where are they?

4. What is the biggest bird in the world?

5. Mercury is the most distant planet from the Sun. True or false?

6. The first person to sail solo around the world could not: a) stop his boat; b) read a map; c) swim.

7. A surprised porcupine fish: a) fills itself with water; b) starts crying; c) explodes.

8. Name six of the nine planets in the Solar System.

9. Most birds die before they are six months old. True or false?

10. The biggest fish on Earth is a type of shark. True or false?

11. Baikal is the name of: a) the longest river on Earth; b) the biggest lake on Earth; c) the oldest ape that ever lived.

12. Where is the thickest skin on your body?

13. What did Yugoslavian air stewardess Vesna Vulovic land in when her plane was blown up in 1972?

14. Which is heavier, the biggest giant saguaro cactus or an elephant?

15. The deep-sea anglerfish has a light-emitting stalk on its: a) tail; b) head; c) bed-side table.

16. Every day, your heart beats: a) about 1,000 times; b) about 10,000 times; c) about 100,000 times.

17. The flower of the rafflesia plant smells of: a) rotting vegetables; b) rotting meat; c) expensive perfume.

18. During your life you can expect to expel 500 bathtubs of urine. True or false?

19. In Japan, macaque monkeys keep warm by wearing coats that they steal from tourists. True or false?

20. A coral reef is made of rock. True or false?

21. The Atacama is: a) the wettest place on Earth; b) the driest desert on Earth; c) the biggest mountain in outer space.

22. The oldest person ever recorded is Jeanne Louise Calment. In which country was she born?

23. A stonefish has poisonous spines on its back. But what does it look like?

24. The planet Pluto is larger than our Moon. True or false?

25. The slowest land mammal on Earth is the: a) sloth; b) proboscis monkey; c) falabella horse.

26. Saturn's rings are made of: a) glass; b) ice, dust and rocks; c) nothing – they are an optical illusion.

27. Where is the biggest wall in the world?

28. What food does the giant panda eat most often?

29. The way Uranus spins is unusual because: a) it doesn't actually spin; b) it spins on its side; c) the speed that it spins depends on how windy it is.

30. The biggest rat-like animal in the world is about the size of an elephant. True or false?

31. Rice is a type of mushroom. True or false?

32. You always sweat, even on cold days. True or false?

33. What is unusual about a puffin's beak?

34. For what purpose does a remora fish use the sucker on its head?

35. The biggest iceberg ever recorded was larger than the European country of Sweden. True or false?

36. The loudest animal on Earth is: a) the blue whale; b) the Savi's pygmy shrew; c) the African elephant.

37. The full name for Krung Thep (also called Bangkok) has 167 letters. But which country is it in?

38. The highest mountains on Earth are in the Himalayas, in Asia. True or false?

39. The architect of the Taj Mahal, in India, was: a) eaten by a Savi's pygmy shrew; b) beheaded; c) tickled to death.

40. The coldest place on Earth is in Ethiopia. True or false?

41. The Gambia is believed to have more bicycles than any other country. True or false?

42. Which ocean is the biggest on Earth?

43. The sundew plant eats: a) insects; b) monkeys; c) bamboo.

44. Which has more bones, a baby human or an adult human?

45. What function does the special gland under a skunk's tail perfom?

46. For albatross chicks to hatch from their eggs, it takes: a) 30 minutes; b) six days; c) six months.

47. What does the volcanic island of Stromboli do almost all of the time?

48. The first ever cycle race was held in: a) Paris, France; b) Madrid, Spain; c) Rome, Italy.

49. Super Frosty was the world's biggest ice-cream cone. True or false?

50. Which country has more roads, the USA or Japan?

Now turn the page to find out how well you did!

Quiz answers

1. Brazil (page 20)
2. b) (page 13)
3. In your ear (page 22)
4. The ostrich (page 15)
5. False (page 4)
6. c) (page 28)
7. a) (page 18)
8. Mercury, Venus, Earth, Mars, Jupiter, Saturn, Uranus, Neptune, Pluto (page 4)
9. True (page 13)
10. True (page 19)
11. b) (page 7)
12. On the soles of your feet (page 25)
13. A pond (page 27)
14. The biggest giant saguaro cactus (page 8)
15. b) (page 18)
16. c) (page 23)
17. b) (page 9)
18. True (page 23)
19. False (page 11)
20. False (page 17)
21. b) (page 6)
22. France (page 26)
23. A weed-covered rock (page 19)
24. False (page 4)
25. a) (page 12)
26. b) (page 5)
27. China (page 27)
28. Bamboo (page 12)
29. b) (page 5)
30. False (page 13)
31. False (page 9)
32. True (page 24)
33. It changes, depending on the time of year (page 14)
34. To attach itself to other fish (page 19)
35. False (page 17)
36. a) (page 10)
37. Thailand (page 21)
38. True (page 7)
39. b) (page 26)
40. False (page 6)
41. False (page 29)
42. The Pacific (page 16)
43. a) (page 9)
44. A baby human (page 22)
45. It produces a vile smell (page 10)
46. b) (page 14)
47. It erupts (page 7)
48. a) (page 29)
49. False (page 27)
50. The USA (page 20)

How did you do?

0-20
Oh dear! Did you read the book before you tried the quiz?

20-24
Perhaps you're just not interested in amazing facts.

25-34
Not bad. You got more than half of the answers right.

35-39
Your score was almost amazing – but not quite!

40-49
You obviously have a good head for amazing facts.

50
Wow! You really know your facts. Well done!

First published in 1996 by Usborne Publishing Ltd, Usborne House, 83-85 Saffron Hill, London EC1N 8RT, England.
Copyright © 1996, 1994, 1992, 1990, 1988, 1987, 1986, Usborne Publishing Ltd.
The name Usborne and the device 🐝 are Trade Marks of Usborne Publishing Ltd.
First published in America March 1997 UE
Printed in Italy